THE LACEYVILLE MONKEYS

Say the Right Words

Dedicated to my beloved mother,
Ethel Silverstein, for her never-ending
inspiration and creativity

H.R.

Published by Illusion Press, LLC
8437 Legend Club Drive
West Palm Beach, Florida 33412
561-775-1652

Library of Congress Control Number: 2009921073

ISBN 978-0-615-26482-0
www.laceyvillemonkeys.com

Design: Maiarelli Studio
Printed in China

THE LACEYVILLE MONKEYS

Say the Right Words

Harriett Ruderman

Illustrations by Beverly Luria

Three little monkeys
came to Laceyville Town
in just the right month
for a night that's renown.

The Big Talent Contest
was coming up soon.
All animals performed
on the eve of full moon.

Owner and trainer
Ms. Hepzibah Mott
had taught her young monkeys
to do quite a lot.

One danced and one sang,
one tumbled and rolled.
Say The Right Words,
watch their talents unfold.

With monkeys in tow,
to Granny's they trot,
a skinny old lady
with hair in a knot.

"We've come for the Contest,"
Hepzibah glowed,
"my monkeys and I
have planned quite a show!"

Granny looked doubtful
for she knew not a bit
of these three little monkeys
with talent and wit.

"What can they do?"
wondered Granny aloud.
"Great talent is needed
for the Laceyville crowd!"

Hepzibah answered,
"These words are their cue
I say them with care …
watch what they do:

"Dance and sing,
Tumble and roll,
Do it with love
Let your magic unfold."

Up went Eva
on tippy toes …
she twirled and she whirled–
she dipped and she rose.

Sheva was next,
he sang like a bird
The prettiest sounds
you've ever heard.

Keva performed
an act of great skill.
He flipped and he tumbled,
giving all a big thrill.

Granny was stunned
her mouth opened wide.
"This incredible act
is amazing!" she cried.

"I'll show off their talents,"
she sneakily thought,
"If I'm clever about it,
I'll never get caught."

So early next evening
from the house the four crept
off to the Contest,
while Hepzibah napped.

The big show began
at the rise of full moon,
when George the Gorilla
played piano and crooned.

Jake the Snake
did a fine cobra dance...

...while Dizzy the Lizard
paraded and pranced.

Bob the Frog
and a Tortoise named Tillie
made everyone laugh—
they were just so silly.

They were all very good
but nothing compared
to the sight that came next
when the monkeys appeared.

Eva was wearing
a tutu of white
with pink ballet slippers,
she looked quite the sight.

Sheva's Tuxedo,
suspenders and tie
gave him a look
that was handsome and sly.

Keva was dressed
in red tights and a tank.
He wore them well
like a star of high rank.

With monkeys on stage
Granny boasted and bragged
how this little group
The Contest would bag.

So eager was Granny
to show off their stuff
she spoke rather harshly,
a little too rough:

"Dance, Sing, and Tumble,"
she shouted aloud.
"Do it right now,
make old Granny proud!"

She prodded and coaxed
she pleaded and begged,
but the monkeys stood silent
for the wrong words were said.

The crowd started laughing
As Granny grew red,
"I'm just so embarrassed,"
the old lady said.

Then out of the blue,
in the midst of their plight,
came Hepzibah Mott,
to save the big night.

"Just wait and see
what my monkeys can do.
When you say these words
there's none like these few."

"Dance a

Tumble an

Do it with

Let your ma

d Sing,

d Roll.

Love

gic unfold."

The talented trio
began to perform
with Hepzibah's words,
so caring and warm.

The townsfolk stood speechless
amazed and entranced
for Eva was doing
a beautiful dance.

Little Sheva sang opera
so sweetly he sounded,
the people swayed softly
completely astounded.

Keva was brilliant.
He tumbled and rolled,
backwards and forwards,
such skill he showed!

The Laceyville folks
went wild with delight.
"Encore!" they shouted,
Oh, what a night!

The monkeys had won
the contest that year,
with this valuable lesson
that Hepzibah shared:

Say the right words
speak kindly to friends,
to family and pets,
the list never ends.

Unlock the magic
Your words are the key
It works every time.
Try it … and see!